Love *and* Disaster *on* Campus

Alfred C. Knoerzer Sr.

Fulton Books
Meadville, PA

Published by Fulton Books 2023

ISBN 979-8-88731-508-9 (paperback)
ISBN 979-8-88731-509-6 (digital)

Printed in the United States of America

DEDICATION

Your author would be grosely remiss if he did not acknowledge the sometimes reluctant enthusiasm when dutifully proofreading portions of what lies between the cover of this book in an effort to give their father an unbiased opinion of the written pages.

Alfred II, the elder of this critical in-house pair, and enthusiastic computer wiz, offered tireless suggestions and corrections to the initial manuscript's content.

Christian J. the author's eighteen year old son, and a musically talented percussionist, offered the author with a teenager's view and some comic relief during otherwise dull or baring periods during your author's brain-dead moments.

Your author's oldest son, though not physically present during this extended period of time, did however offer continuous encouragement to his aging father through phone calls and correspondence during the entire writing process.

My tireless, caring wife, Maritess, proved to be the inspiration and indispensable glue which held all these various efforts together and on track.

Your author gratefully acknowledges his sincere thanks and appreciation...

CONTENTS

CHAPTER 1

The Beginnings

Terry "Twinkles" Booker waited patiently at the newly installed traffic light at the corner of Fourth and Mail in this small college town of White Hill, Indiana. Traffic was just starting to build on this first day of fall semester registration for the college school year 1976–77.

At the changing of the traffic light in Terry's favor, the attractive young lady in her red Jeep prepared to enter the intersection. Suddenly a speeding car in the cross street sped through the intersection, trying to beat the light, cutting just in front of Twinkles. Fortunately, Twinkles saw the light-running car with its smiling and waving driver, in time to stop.

Luckily for Twinkles and the driver behind her, that driver was also watching the traffic and managed to stop her vehicle before running into Twinkles's Jeep.

After giving a *thank-you* wave to the driver in the car behind her, Twinkles moved on through the intersection and on to her destination at the local college.

Still a little shaken by the very recent traffic incident, the young lady sat in her Jeep in the college parking lot for several minutes until she had calmed down.

Once sufficiently relaxed, the petite five-foot-four-inch senior student put the near accident behind her and concentrated on entering Indiana Normal College.

The registration line was long and slow-moving, causing Twinkles to seriously consider leaving the building and trying her luck later in the day.

Just as she was about to leave, a very familiar voice called out to her.

"Twinkles, what are you doing over there?" Cindy called out. "Come on to the cafeteria with me. I have someone I want you to meet. You can come back here later when the line will be shorter."

Quickly Twinkles followed her friend out of the registration area and into the adjoining cafeteria, where an unfamiliar young man sat patiently waiting.

As the students approached the table where the young man waited, he stood up and offered a warm smile.

"Twinkles, this is Howard," Cindy announced. "He is a transfer student from a college in Las Vegas, Nevada, no less. He will be joining us here in Indiana for the current year."

While the three students were getting seated, Twinkles turned to Cindy and remarked, "My, you have been a busy little beaver, haven't you?"

Cindy blushed easily as both Twinkles and Howard enjoyed a good laugh as a third young lady joined the happy group.

"Why all the laughter?" the newcomer inquired. "This is registration day. I thought laughter was reserved for graduation day."

"Well, this is sort of a special occasion," Cindy explained. "We have a new friend joining us today. His first name is Howard. We haven't known him long enough to learn his last name yet. See how new he is?"

Turning to Howard, Cindy announced. "Howard, this is Alice. Alice, this is Howard. I would tell you his last name, but unfortunately, I don't know it. That lets you know just how new he is here."

"Nice to meet you, Alice," Howard said as he offered his hand to Alice. "And I do have a last name. It is Williams."

Accepting her new friend's hand, Alice offered, "Welcome to Indiana Normal. We may not be as big as Indiana U., but we are just as proud to be carrying our state's name."

"Well said," Howard came back. "Are you a politics major?" he asked as everyone laughed.

Changing the subject and his attention to Twinkles, Howard repeated her name, "Twinkles." Then he ventured, "There has to be a story in there somewhere."

"You can blame it on my father," Twinkles started. "It all started when I was just a baby. He said that whenever I smiled, my eyes would sparkle. He figured that he could not name his new baby *Sparkles*, so he gave me the nickname of Twinkles, and it has stuck with me ever since."

"I'll bet you were a beautiful baby too," Howard remarked as he winked at Cindy.

Turning to Allice, Twinkles quickly joked, "You had better be careful around this one," as she playfully nodded at Howard.

"I'm not worried about that. I've got my Freddy," Alice replied.

"That's right," Twinkles confirmed. "Her boyfriend is six feet, eight inches tall and the star of our basketball team. Last spring he scored forty-eight points over a major college team in the state's semi-finals in Indianapolis."

"That's pretty impressive," Howard concluded.

Then changing the subject to his own interests, Howard asked, "Do you have a debating team here?"

"Yes, indeed," Alice responded. "Are you a debater?"

"Captain of our college team in Vegas," he boasted.

"This is great," Twinkles exclaimed excitedly. "We can have our own in-house debates. Frankly, a couple of our current debate members are not that hot."

"I look forward to such a debate," Howard acknowledged.

Twinkles then leaned closer to Cindy and whispered, just loud enough so that everyone else at the small table could hear her, "We think he is single and still available."

"You girls don't waste any time, do you?" Howard joked.

Howard asked, "Do you have any good sports teams here?"

"You don't know much about Indiana, do you? Indiana is basketball heaven."

"You don't say?" Howard replied tongue in cheek.

"Surely you have to know something about our fine state?" Cindy teased.

"Not really. I'm from New Port, Rhode Island, you know," Howard teased.

"You mean that you have never been to the Indianapolis Motor Speedway?"

"No," he calmly replied.

"Notre Dame Stadium?"

"Not that I know of."

"The Indiana Pacer?"

"Who are they?" Now he was just having fun with her.

"Where have you been liking?" she asked. "Under a rock?"

"Well, there is one bright spot waiting in my future," he admitted.

"Next year, my father has me lined up to attend Purdue University's School of Engineering."

"It's about time," Twinkles concurred. "We may get you educated yet."

"This is quite a change from Vegas," Howard commented. "Do you have any other sports teams here?"

"Of course," Twinkles replied. "County champs in football. We have several big, tall guys, mostly farm boys, who can really hold their own against those big city guys. Our real power is in our basketball team," added Cathy. "But Alice is more qualified to talk about that."

"Why is that?" Howard wanted to know.

"Because she has been dating the star player for the last two years."

"Freddy is our local star, but not only because of his height. He is a talented player and a good team leader. When you meet him, you will see that he is a fun guy, but when he steps onto the court, he is all business."

"You should think about a career in sports broadcasting."

"As they say, 'this has been fun,' and I am looking forward to more chats with all of you in the coming weeks. Right now, my ride should be waiting, and I must be getting back to my hotel."

With Howard's departure, the small group of happy enrollees started heading their separate ways, vowing to meet again in the morrow.

CHAPTER 2

Shantelle

Freddy pulled his used Mercury into an open spot near the front of the administration building just in time to see Twinkles and an unfamiliar man enter the science building.

He had an impulse to call out to her but then changed his mind. There would be ample time to ask her about that later in the day. The good friends were scheduled to meet in the cafeteria after they had completed locking in their individual schedules.

The lobby of the small snack bar was quite crowded, and it took several minutes for Freddy to locate his friends.

As he spotted Alice, he noticed that she was seriously engaged in conversation with a person he had not seen before.

Since the two young women were involved in a conversation, Freddy decided to stand back for a minute or two. That new lady talking with Alice was quite attractive and well-dressed. *A new entry into our happy campus*, he thought to himself.

She is dressed more like a professor than a student, Freddy mused to himself. *I'll have to ask Alice about her later on.*

Seeing that Alice had noticed him standing there, Freddy quickly approached their table, where the ladies were waiting.

"Been waiting long?" he asked as he approached.

"Not really," Alice replied. "I have been getting acquainted with our new friend, Shantelle. Shantelle, this is my good friend, Freddy."

"My, you are a tall one," the young lady replied.

"Six foot, eight." Alice proudly answered for the college basketball player. "He led our team to a key victory by scoring forty-eight points in a championship game last season."

"Tall and talented too," the lady admitted.

Truly Freddy was an impressive fixture in this small Indiana town.

"And how about you?" Freddy asked, turning all the attention onto their new friend.

"I'm afraid I don't have much to tell. I'm just an ordinary college student, like the rest of you."

She may be new here, Freddy said to himself, *but she sure isn't ordinary.*

"By the way, your name is Shantelle, right? Isn't that French? That is such a pretty name," Freddy commented.

"Why, thank you, Freddy. I appreciate that. Is everyone in this town so nice?"

"No, really," Alice replied. "You just happened to catch us on a lucky day."

Shantelle was quick to catch Alice's sly sense of humor. "It sounds like this is a very happy campus."

"Oh yah," Freddy cut in. "Just wait until you have a class under Old Man Rushcroft. He'll bring you back to reality real quick."

"Seriously, though," Freddy leaned back in his chair and asked, "and we ask this of everyone who shows up at Indiana Normal. What in the world ever possessed you to come here? Especially when we have illustrious universities such as Notre Dame and Indiana U. to choose from."

"It's a long story," Shantelle started, "but I'll try to make it brief. My professor from last year used to teach at this college some years ago, and he was worried about all the distractions that I encountered at my old school in Los Angeles, and he told me that I should get away from all those big university distractions and transfer to a smaller college away from all that rat race."

"And were you terribly distracted back there?" Alice wanted to know.

"You wouldn't believe," Shantelle relayed. "It was party after party. One fun night after another. I really hand it to those guys who stick to their books and get the job done."

"I can imagine," Freddy cut in, just before receiving a sharp kick in the ankle from under the table.

"I kid you not," their new friend continued. "It is hard to concentrate on your studies in an environment like that. So now, here I am in a small town, Indiana, all thanks to Professor Tonner."

"Not bald-headed Thurm Tonner?" Alice and Freddy asked, almost in unison.

"Don't tell me you know him?" Shantelle asked in disbelief.

"Know him? No. Know of him? Yes. He is a legend around here," Alice confirmed.

"If you tell your professor here that you actually know Old Professor Tonner, you will have a friend here for life," Freddy confirmed.

"Getting back to your French name…"

CHAPTER 3

Aunt Millie and the Charger

It was a Sunday, much like any other Sunday, except that the fourth-year college student was scanning the classified ads of the local Sunday paper for car sales ads.

Burt Nickels was especially looking at the *auto* section for a possible upgrade to replace his mostly unreliable current ride.

With the extra money he was receiving from his current part-time job at *Ecco Electronics and More*, he was now able to upgrade.

As he neared the end of his fruitless search, a small classified ad caught his eye.

"Dependable, low-mileage Dodge in good shape $1,000 or best offer." There was only one other item besides the phone number. It reads, "Cash only."

The excited young man grabbed a pen, and on the back of a used envelope, he wrote down the phone number. The lady who answered the phone call said that he was the first caller and that she would hold the car for him if he could come to look at the car before 3:00 p.m., just in case she had other callers.

Just as Burt was about to head for his car, a sudden thought crossed his mind.

I wonder if Twinkles would like a Sunday ride in the country? Why not give it a try? he asked himself.

Twinkles was still lounging around when her bedside private phone line sprang to life.

Sleepily the awakened lady reached for her phone as she wondered who would call her on a Sunday morning.

"Burt?" she questioned. "What's up? This is Sunday, you know."

Her friend was quick to recognize the half sleep in her voice.

"Hey, sleepy," came Burt's response. "Why don't you get up and do something for a change? I have to take a drive in the country this morning. Why don't you rub the sleep out of your eyes and ride along? I might even buy you a frappuccino."

"In the country? Why?" she asked in quick succession.

"Can't tell you," he quipped. "It's classified. I can only tell you in person."

Burt knew that he was playing on Twinkles's secret passion for solving riddles, and it worked.

"All right, Burt," she replied. "You are impossible. Give me a half hour to get dressed."

"No can do," he came back, sounding very mysterious. "This is top secret stuff. I'll be in your driveway in twelve minutes."

The steady tone of the phone let Twinkles know that he was not taking *no* for an answer.

As expected, Burt's friend stepped out onto the Booker family front porch just as Burt pulled his car into the driveway. If nothing else, Twinkles was never late, for anything.

"So where are we going on this supersecret mission?" the curious friend inquired.

"I am going to introduce you to an old friend of mine," he teased.

Sensing Burt's teasing nature, Twinkles shot back, "And for this, I gave up my Sunday morning sleep-in? I sure hope that she is worth it."

"Oh, you'll love her. I just know it," he responded.

"Probably not half as much as you will."

"All I ask," he continued, "is just keep an open mind and be nice to her. She has a delicate condition."

"Well, if she is interested in you, her condition is probably mental."

As Burt pulled into the long winding driveway, Twinkles sat up and began to show interest in his secret destination. This was the Bradshaws' small country farm.

Twinkles had not been with Burt when he first drove to Aunt Millie's farm a year earlier.

The elderly, but spry, woman was waiting on the front porch of the farmhouse. The smiling woman immediately recognized Burt from his earlier visit to buy some auto parts from Mr. Bradshaw a year earlier.

Suddenly remembering the passing of her husband some months earlier, Burt sincerely expressed his condolences and asked how she was getting along on the farm all alone.

"Oh, I have lots of friends here, and George Hackins from down the road has agreed to farm this small place for two-fifths of the year's net profits."

"Did you ever think about moving into town, Aunt Millie?"

"Not really. Mr. Bradshaw would want me to stay in the old place here. It's the only home I've known for over forty years."

"Mr. Bradshaw was a fine man," Burt acknowledged, bringing a smile to the woman's face.

"That he was, son. Nice of you to remember him."

"I remember the last time I was here," Burt recalled. "Once we finished our business, he brought out that bottle of Jose Cuervo. We sat and talked and must have finished half of that bottle."

"I still have the rest of that bottle on the shelf. You are welcome to take it with you. The good Lord knows that I will never drink it," the kind lady offered.

"Heavens no, Aunt Millie," Burt quickly responded. "That Indiana highway patrol would have me in jail by sundown."

"Well, look at my manners, leaving your pretty wife standing out there while I just run on about everything," Aunt Millie scolded herself.

During this whole banter back and forth between Aunt Millie and Burt, Twinkles had been standing there, smiling and enjoying the happy chitchat, secretly marveling how casual and polite he was to the elderly lady when all he was here for was to look at a used car.

Maybe I should start looking at Burt a little more closely, she quietly said to herself.

"Thanks, Aunt Millie," Burt remarked. "But she is not my wife."

"And we are not planning on it either," Twinkles added.

"I'll never understand this modern generation," Aunt Millie mumbled to herself. Then out loud she added, "But you two look like such a lovely couple."

"Sorry to disappoint you, Aunt Millie, but I could never put up with this guy for life," Twinkles added.

"We are just friends," Burt explained.

"And classmates at the college in town," Twinkles quickly added.

"Well, you came out here to look at a car," the talkative lady said, "and so you shall. It is in the garage behind the house, along with a lot of other stuff."

"Aunt Millie was not lying," Burt whispered to his friend as they approached the opened garage door.

It was clear to Burt that this was not going to be easy.

"Aunt Millie, are you sure that there is a car in here?"

"Oh yes," she quickly replied. "I watched the Willson boys put it in there. I remember that Billy Willson had to climb through a window to get himself out. That is because I didn't want to see it again after Mr. Bradshaw passed away."

Burt was beginning to worry about the condition of the car, with all the stuff she had the brothers pile on top of it.

After twenty minutes of removing boxes, blankets, and other stuff off the still-hidden vehicle, the general shape of the car was revealed, sort of. There was still an old blanket covering the object of their search.

After taking a deep breath, Burt gently peeled back the dusty blanket. Still holding the end of the blanket, Burt could hardly believe his own eyes.

What Aunt Millie had simply described as an old Dodge turned out to be a 1966 Dodge Charger.

Burt felt guilty as he counted out the ten fresh $100 bills that he had withdrawn from his savings account the day before, on the off chance that he could find a suitable car that weekend.

Burt told Aunt Millie that the car was probably worth more than that, but she just told him, "A deal is a deal. I'm just happy to have it out of here."

It was obvious to Burt that it was going to take too much time—and effort—to get it that same day, saying, "I will need some very hefty help to get this out of here."

Turning to the sweet lady, he asked, "Can I leave this car here for a few days? I will need to get some help to get this car out here."

"Of course, you can, Burt," she replied. "I already have the money. It is your car now. I have the title in the house. Let me get it for you."

"Thanks, Aunt Millie. I'll get some help in a few days while I figure out if it is drivable. And we will put your garage back in order."

"Take as much time as you need. I'm not going anywhere."

On the way back to town, Twinkles remarked, "You were right, Burt. Aunt Millie is a very nice lady."

CHAPTER 4

Burt and Freddy Car Talk

Whil Twinkles and Howard were discussing modern music, Burt and his buddy were discussing autos and particularly the classic Dodge Charger that Burt had just purchased from Aunt Millie.

Burt was trying hard to hide his obvious excitement over actually finding a Charger in such a short time.

"And she let you have it for only ten grand?" Freddy tried hard to appear properly impressed. Actually Freddy had not really heard nor read about the Charger, which had its hay day some ten years earlier.

"Let me tell you, Freddy," Burt eagerly continued. "The Charger was the classic car of the '60s. I actually drove one three years ago when I visited my cousin in Chicago. He had one in black. It was the boss car of its time. Advanced styling, a powerful V8 engine—426 *Hemi*, stick shift, fastback styling, it's awesome!"

"When am I going to see this beauty?" Freddy asked, showing more enthusiasm now.

"That is why I called you here tonight," Burt explained. "I can drive that classic, but I need you to help me put it all back in perfect order."

"Now that is a pretty tall order, buddy," Freddy admitted. "I'd have to get a good look at it first. If it has been sitting undriven for a long time, it might not even run anymore."

14

"That is why I need your help. You know cars. Your brother even has a car shop in town. I know how to drive cars and how to appreciate fine cars, but I know very little about how to fix cars. I want to take you to Aunt Millie's farm this weekend and have you take a good look at this machine. Tell me you are free this Sunday."

"Well, I was planning to go skydiving this weekend," Freddy joked, "but I guess I could postpone that."

"Seriously," Burt pleaded. "Can you help me?"

"Seriously," his friend replied. "Yes, I can. After hearing you go on and on about this classic, I can't wait to see it. You can pick me up around nine, and you can show me where this place is," Freddy replied.

"No, that won't work," Burt replied. "If by some chance the car is drivable, I can drive it back here, and you can follow me, just in case it doesn't make it."

"Doesn't sound so encouraging to me," Freddy quipped.

"Just pick me up at my place around nine o'clock Sunday morning," Burt replied.

"Any other business before we adjourn?" Freddy asked.

"Not unless you have time for a quick beer," Burt offered.

"I guess I could find enough time for just one," his friend conceded.

"You get the beer mugs while I get the beer," Burt commanded.

"Righto, Captain," came Freddy's quick reply.

CHAPTER 5

Freddy Drinks
Wine with Shantelle

As Freddy entered the campus side general store, which, oddly enough, goes by the name the *Campus Side General Store*, to his surprise, he spotted his new friend, Miss Shantelle, in the checkout line.

Having an opportunity to speak with her alone, so to speak, was a situation he had not anticipated.

"What a pleasant surprise," Freddy greeted his new friend. "Finding everything you are looking for? I've been in here so often over the past three years that I can find almost anything, even blindfolded," he joked.

"That's awfully kind of you, Freddy," she replied. "I'm just picking up a few odds and ends for my new apartment."

"Did you find a place here, near the campus?"

"Yes, and only about a block and a half from campus."

"That's really lucky. Most of us have places as much as a mile away, and still the price is high."

Then changing the subject, he asked, "Did you find a roommate yet, you know, to help with the rent?"

"No," came the quick reply. "And I'm not really looking for one, at least not now. I'm used to having my own space, and the rent is really not that high, especially when you compare it to what I was paying last year in Los Angeles."

Spotting an open checkout counter, Shantelle quickly remarked, "There's an open lane. Let's grab it."

Pausing their easy conversation while going through the checkout lane, Freddy noticed that some of her grocery items were mostly diet or low-cal items.

"Don't tell me that you are on a diet?" Freddy teased.

"A woman has to maintain that girlish figure, you know," the stunning brunette replied.

"It looks like your figure is in pretty good shape already," her helpful companion replied.

"Why, thank you for noticing," she came back, along with a wink.

"Let me help you to your car," Freddy offered as he carried her two bags of groceries.

"Oh, I don't have a car yet. I'm planning on taking care of that this weekend. Maybe you could help me, if it's not a bother. I know cars, but I don't know the car dealers in this town."

"You planning to walk to your place with these groceries? No way. I can pack them for you. I wasn't doing anything important anyway," he explained.

"Well, thanks again," the attractive lady replied.

"Anything to help a pretty lady," Freddy said with a smile.

"Why, Freddy," she replied with a wink. "If I didn't know you better and also know about that pretty young lady you were with the other day, I'd think that you were flirting with me."

"Now, Shantelle," he replied. "I'm only expressing what I'm seeing."

"This is my building." Shantelle pointed out. "You can give me those bags now. My apartment is on the second floor."

"No way for that to happen," Freddy announced. "These bags are too heavy. I can carry them up for you. Besides, how can you unlock your door while holding two big sacks of groceries?"

"Okay," she consented, "but I'll give you a quick drink as a means of payment, for being such a sweet guy."

"Agreed," Freddy remarked, as he followed her up the steel outdoor steps to the second-floor landing. With a massive effort, Freddy resisted the temptation to look up.

As Shantelle unlocked the door and stepped inside, she called out to Freddy to please put the packages on an end table near a very comfortable-looking couch near the door.

"This is a really nice apartment." The young man observed as he turned around to get a quick survey of the large room. "This is nothing like the places where I live."

"It is doable," she replied with an air of mere acceptance, leaving the impression that she was accustomed to nicer accommodations.

"Can you give me a hand here?" came the call from the adjoining kitchen area.

Freddy entered the small kitchen area to see Shantelle standing on a kitchen chair while trying to balance two cocktail glasses in one hand and an empty ice bucket in the other hand.

Just as this star NCAA basketball player entered the room, one of the cocktail glasses slipped from Shantelle's grasp and started on its long downward trip to certain destruction, when a large athletic hand temporarily stopped its fall. With the fragile glass too far out of Freddy's grasp, he simply used the tip of his long finger to tip the glass into the air and then inched closer to the refalling object and firmly, but gently, grasp the spinning object with his full right hand, thus avoiding a dangerous and troublesome broken glass cleanup.

"Wow," the surprised young lady exclaimed. "That was amazing. You sure are a quick thinker."

"Thinking had nothing to do with it," Freddy calmly explained. "When there is not enough time to think, your trained reflexes take over. Often that can mean the difference between being an NBA starter or a guy sitting at the end of the bench most of the season."

Gingerly Shantelle took the unbroken glass from Freddy's hand and gently placed it on the kitchen table.

Turning to Freddy, she asked, "Care for a cocktail after that performance?"

"Sorry to refuse your offer, but I'm a B and B man."

"And what in the world is that?" she asked with a grin.

"Beer and bourbon" was the quick, but polite, reply.

"Well, I don't have any of that, but I do have some fine wine."

"Now that I can handle, but only one. I'm drivin', you know."

"It's a deal then."

Shantelle was finding Freddy to be a very enjoyable friend and drinking partner, but the image of him and Alice together kept coming back to her mind. She decided that she should move cautiously on this situation. It wouldn't be wise to settle into local love affairs until she had a better understanding of the "lay of the land," so to speak.

There would be time for Freddy, if the opportunity ever arose. For now she decided to just keep it light.

True to his word, after one glass of local liquor-store wine, Freddy left Shantelle's apartment amid thoughts of *What if...*

Graduation was still nearly nine months away. A lot can happen in nine months.

CHAPTER 6

Twinkles Welcomes
a New Student

Twinkles arrived especially early this morning because she real-ized seating spaces would be hard to find on this first day of regular classes here in the fall term at Indiana Normal College.

Twinkles's self-prediction of the crowded condition inside the college cafeteria proved to be true. Thoughts of facing this hectic day without her regular cup of espresso brought a frown to her otherwise pretty face, until a familiar voice caught her attention.

It was Howard Williams at a small corner table raising his hand and motioning to an empty chair.

Quickly moving to the waiting chair, Twinkles smiled and asked what brought him out so early this morning.

"I'm an early bird," he replied easily, as he allowed himself a few seconds to savor the fine looks of his new friend. Although he fully appreciated this young lady's small-town innocent looks, this more worldly young man decided to "file away" such remarks until a more appropriate time, if an occasion ever arose.

"I am pleasantly surprised by the fragmented arrangement of this campus—one building here, another one there."

"It is not by design. I can assure you," Twinkles replied. "Just wait until you have one class on the second floor of one building and the next class a block away."

"But seriously, why would anyone leave Vegas for this small-town campus?"

"To be honest," he confessed, "craps."

"Pardon?" the surprised young lady replied. "Did I hear you say *crabs*?"

"No, no," Howard came back with a laugh. "I said *craps*, like the table game in gambling."

"So you are a gambler?" the young lady asked cautiously.

"That's right," he confessed. "And I make no secret of it. It is a curse I'm saddled with. It is that tantalizing feeling that the next throw of the dice could make me rich."

"Do you always lose?" Twinkles asked.

"Not really," Howard admitted. "And that is the main problem," he added. "If I always lost, it would make it much easier to stop. But once you have hit that first big win, you start believing that the 'next' roll of the dice will be another big win. But that doesn't happen very often.

"A rare dealer with whom I became a good friend told me to get far away from Vegas, or I would soon wind up like the panhandlers, who ask you for money every time you get into your car to leave.

"So that's my sad story of how I got here," Howard related. "I hope your story is a little happier."

"Well, at least mine is not so tragic," Twinkles came back. "I didn't come here from anywhere."

With a puzzled look, Howard inquired, "How was that?"

"I didn't come here from anywhere because I was born here. Can't get much more local than that," she explained.

"Good one," he replied with an easy smile.

CHAPTER 7

Cindy Sees Freddy at Shantelle's Apt.

As Cindy approached Shantelle's apartment building from a dimly lit side street, she noticed someone who resembled Freddy coming down the outside stairs from Shantelle's apartment.

As the man passed under the corner streetlight, Cindy was almost sure that it was Freddy. Cindy was tempted to call out to her friend but decided against it. There would be time enough tomorrow to mention it to him.

Crossing the same street, Cindy quickly climbed the same metal stairs leading to Shantelle's apartment.

Shantelle, who was in the process of washing two freshly used wineglasses, interrupted her glass cleaning and moved the few short steps to the apartment door, where she greeted her new friend.

After inviting Cindy to just lay her light jacket on the nearby chair, Shantelle quickly thanked her friend for dropping off the requested textbook, *Changing Social Patterns*.

With a sarcastic grin, Shantelle inquired, "Was the book filled with new and uplifting ideas?"

"Now wouldn't that be a pleasant surprise?" her friend ventured. "It was just more of the same old worn-out ideas dressed up in a shiny new book cover."

"Why can't males realize that women know how to think on their own and develop their own ideas and interpretations of events," Shantelle offered.

"We should be so lucky," Cindy replied, matching her new friend's level of sarcasm.

"Anyway, thanks for the loan," Shantelle acknowledged again.

Suddenly changing the subject, Shantelle asked with a smile, "Can I offer you a glass of wine on this chilly evening? I was just about to put it back after sharing a glass of it with my visitor."

"Was that visitor Freddy?" Cindy asked with a cautious smile and one raised eyebrow.

"Why, yes," Shantelle admitted. "He is such a dear. He ran into me at the variety store, where I was buying some groceries, and as usual, I wound up buying more than I could carry. Freddy offered to carry them for me, so I offered him a glass of wine for his trouble. And after just one glass, he excused himself and left."

"Just out of curiosity, is there anything serious going on between him and that girl, Alice?"

"I'm afraid so," her new friend replied. "Alice has had that relationship locked up pretty solid for the past two years."

"Can't say that I blame her," Shantelle regretted.

"As for the glass of wine," Cindy offered, "I'll gladly take a rain check on that. Tonight I have some heavy reading to do, and wine makes my eyes get fuzzy."

"It's a deal, anytime," Shantelle offered as she followed her friend to the door.

It was the following morning, as Cindy entered the half-filled classroom, where she saw Alice waiting for her. Alice had placed her jacket on the seat of the chair next to her as a way of reserving it for her classmate.

"I saved you a seat because the room is starting to fill up," Alice remarked.

"Thanks," Cindy responded as she settled in. "Are you ready for this hour-long lecture?"

"Fully prepared," her friend answered as she pulled back the corner of a neat hankie, revealing a bulky, but effective, tape recorder. "Cost me a small fortune, but it will be worth it."

With wide-open eyes, Cindy quickly but quietly asked, "Why didn't you tell me about this? I could have slept for an extra hour."

"I had to check it out on my own first," Alice replied. "I had to make sure it would actually record. This is cutting-edge setup, you know."

"Well," Cindy cut in with an "I know something you don't know" grin, looking strangely like the cat who ate the cannery.

"And does this bit of information involve me?" Alice inquired.

"Directly, no, but indirectly, yes indeed."

"Are you going to tell me something, or are we going to sit here and play guessing games?" Alice was tired of games and of this one, in particular.

"Okay," Cindy relented. "I went to Shantelle's place last night to give her a book that she will need next sem. It is on a subject that we have both completed."

"And?" Alice pressed on.

"Just as I was approaching the building, I saw Freddy leaving her apartment."

"Are you sure? And you think it was Freddy?"

"Not think, I know it was Freddy. He passed directly under a streetlight," Cindy confirmed.

Why would Freddy be in her apartment, and at night? the troubled young lady wondered, mostly to herself.

"Shantelle said it was because Freddy helped her carry her groceries home from the store," then she added, "As a thank-you, Shantelle offered him a glass of wine."

As Cindy ended her sentence, Professor Kingman called for order in the classroom, and all students fell silent, all students except Alice, who leaned close to Cindy and whispered, "You and I will talk after class."

There was no need for a response from Cindy. The comment was more of an order than a suggestion.

CHAPTER 8

A Cool October Night

It was late October, and the nearly full moon showed brightly in the evening sky. The two college students, walking leisurely across the college campus, did not seem to mind the crisp evening air.

Twinkles held on to Howard, inquiring about her friend's financial plans for after graduation next spring. He had been quite open about his family and their business ventures but spoke very little about his own goals, except for plans for advanced studies in engineering at Purdue University next fall. As for long-term goals, he was pretty much tied to the goals that his father had already laid out for him in his father's corporation.

Once before, Twinkles had inquired about this next phase in his studies, and it seemed to hit a tender spot with him. But now that graduation was only seven months away, Twinkles thought that she would try again, especially if she was beginning to think about a serious relationship. Once again the serious conversation seemed to make him close up about the topic.

"First of all, I have to pass all my current subjects and with high grades," he replied.

Twinkles quickly realized that this was an obvious side step to avoid the question. *Surely the hesitation cannot be financial,* Twinkles told herself silently.

"Does your decision require 'Daddy's' approval?" The lady just could not resist an opportunity to needle him about his money.

"That is one thing that most of you people cannot get straight," he responded.

"Just because you see me spending money freely here, you all think that I am rich. Well, I'm not. My father is rich. I'm only living off his money. I won't be rich until I can do these things with my own money. That is a big difference," he concluded.

"Sorry," Twinkles quickly replied. "I just thought…"

"I just thought," he broke in with a mocking tone. "You thought that because he is rich, then I am rich too. Well, it doesn't work that way. A man is not rich until *he* makes himself rich. My father told me those words a thousand times," he continued.

Again, Twinkles replied, "I didn't mean to embarrass you."

"Well, you did not," he said calmly. "It is just something that I have to deal with, again and again."

"We'll not mention it again," she replied. "So you are planning on staying in Indiana for a while?" she questioned.

"As it stands right now," he answered, "or he may call tomorrow and change my plans."

"It must be frustrating, living your life like that," she said.

"You have no idea," Howard came back.

"Let's change the subject," the young lady repeated.

"Fine," he agreed.

"How about sports?" she offered.

"Don't play it, except for fencing. Now fencing is a highly valuable sport," he continued, more excited now. "It teaches balance, poise, strategy, and quick reactions."

"Sounds like you know a lot about the sport," Twinkles remarked, showing a keen interest in the sport. "Do you participate actively?" Then without waiting for an answer, she rushed on to her next question, "One part of fencing that I don't understand. I have seen a few of those matches on TV, and one thing bothered me about the sport."

"What could that be?" Howard asked while trying hard not to smile at the question he was sure was coming.

"When the match is over, the men never come out and take their shirts off, so we can't really tell."

"Tell you what, my dear little Twinkles?" Howard asked with a hint of a smile beginning to show.

"When they are fencing out there, do they really stab each other with those long sharp swords or sabers?"

The raw childlike innocence in Twinkles's eyes, as she asked Howard the question, was a mood-changing event. The serious man laughed as he folded her into his arms.

"Twinkles, maybe your daddy was a little bit wrong when he named you *Twinkles*. I think he could have named you *Precious*."

Being held tightly like this suddenly gave a whole new perspective to this relationship. But that sudden burst of genuine laughter brought to life another aspect of Howard's personality.

At heart, this was a very serious man, with little time for fun or laughter.

Twinkles could see only two options *if* she were to go ahead with this affair.

First of all, Howard, from all appearances, seemed to be a serious, steadfast man, with little appetite for change.

This situation leaves Twinkles with two choices:

1) Try to change him if you feel you can.
2) Accept him as he is and change yourself.

CHAPTER 9

The Blame Game

Softly Burt looked down at the lovely young lady curled up beside him on the front seat of his like-new car.

The sky was clear, displaying a million stars. The mood in the car was light and soothing, as these two friends shared an infrequent, but appreciated, evening together.

It had been a pleasant evening for two young lovers sharing life together without words to mess things up.

Although this was two romantic people, this was not a romantic couple. This was the case of two very close friends passing time by enjoying an evening star show in the early darkness.

Burt had parked his car on a small incline near the end of an empty parking lot. From here the entire southern sky was clearly visible.

At the young man's suggestion, the two friends got out of the car to get an even better view.

To Burt's way of thinking, this was stargazing at its best.

While the setting was perfect for romantic exchanges, the two viewers were, personally, looking in two different directions.

The young lady was looking at the debris of a love gone wrong, while the young man was looking forward to what he dreamed could be a successful love relationship with the lady by his side.

But for all his dreams and expectations, he was, at heart, a realist. As such, he only allowed himself these momentary lapses into the fantasy world. For Burt, the whole near-perfect experience was really only a temporary glimpse of that "what if" world where he could imagine real-life experiences while realizing that such wonders were left for other mortals to enjoy.

Twinkles, on the other hand, was revisiting the wreckage of another failed love affair. *Why does it always end like this?* she wondered. *Will Howard be another?*

Both of her last affairs appeared to be the perfect fit, only to fall apart when "push came to shove" in both of these relationships.

Finally coming out of her reverie, Twinkles calmly asked, "Think it is time for us to be getting back to reality?"

"Good point," Burt replied. "I guess we both kind of drifted off."

"Are you going to check out that speaker on 'runaway military spending' tomorrow?" Twinkles asked. "I think the military budget is getting way out of control."

"I think I need to concentrate more on my own budget."

"I'll fill you in if there is anything worth repeating," she replied as they both climbed back into Burt's dream car.

As the couple settled back into the car again, Twinkles again move close to Burt and rested her head against Burt's right arm. She was beginning to wonder, *What if…*

Burt shifted his position slightly to steer the car more easily, and Twinkles asked, "Am I interfering with your driving? I can sit up straight."

"Not at all," he quickly replied. "Just make yourself comfortable. I'll have us back to your house in no time."

Twinkles gave her driver a soft warm smile, which Burt interpreted to mean "I need you in my life, and I think I love you."

Encouraged by the smile and the closeness of his longtime friend, the mistaken young man decided to try his hand at charming his companion. He slowed down the car and reached over, to give Twinkles a soft, but firm, hug, while keeping one eye on the deserted country road.

Twinkles's reaction was to force herself free and remark, "Burt, watch your driving."

"I was just testing a theory of mine about your dating pattern."

"You were testing my *what!*" she exclaimed.

"Well," he calmly began. "You have had two serious relation-ships in the past year."

"So what," came the indignant reply.

Twinkles was more than a little concerned as to where this conversation was headed.

Brushing the woman's question aside, he continued, "One was the son of a business tycoon, and the other was a sharp, but slightly immature, possibility. What is the similarity between these two men? You, yourself, said that they both were really fine prospects."

"So you think that this is my fault?" she asked in disbelief.

Twinkles was sitting fully upright now and moving to the far side of that wide front seat.

A look of disbelief now took over where that sweet smile was showing only moments before.

"You think that this is all my fault, don't you? Just whose side are you on here?"

"It's not a matter of taking sides, Twinkles," he replied. "I'm only suggesting that we take a close look at both sides of this," Burt was trying to ease himself out of a tight spot of his own making.

"What side? There is only one side here. *My side!*"

Burt quickly realized that he was on the wrong side of a very personal argument. This was totally new territory for this pair.

"Let's just calmly look at what just happened here," he started. Burt realized that he had already taken this conversation too far for him to back out now.

"I don't think I want to hear any more of your ideas. You just sit here and talk about all the things that you think I've been wrong about."

Looking up, Twinkles suddenly realized that during their intense discussion, the pair had reached the Booker driveway and Burt had turned off the car.

Realizing that her escape from this unpleasant situation was at hand, Twinkles firmly declared, "I've heard enough. I'm getting out!"

As Twinkles turned to get out of the car, Burt took hold of her left hand and stopped her.

"Let go of my hand. You're hurting me!" she exclaimed.

The girl's escape plan had not worked, as Burt gently eased her back into the car.

Changing his approach to a more mellow tone, Burt urged, "Come on, Twinkles, we have come a long way together as best friends. There is nothing that we cannot talk about. Give me three minutes, and then I'll leave, and you will never have to talk to me again."

"Look at me," he quietly asked. "After all those years, surely I'm worth three minutes of your time."

Twinkles pulled her hand away from her dear friend and looked directly at him and said, "Go ahead. You have three minutes, and the clock is already running."

Silent, Burt held back an impulse to smile at Twinkles as they sat in the front seat of that car but then realized the seriousness of the moment.

"Twinkles," he softly started. The young man realized that he had muffed his first attempt at smoothing things over with his friend. He also knew that if he blew his second attempt, he would not likely ever get a third chance to set things right between them.

"Twinkles," he restarted. "We have been through a lot together. I have always tried to be there for you, even if I didn't like what you were about to do. I gave you my best decision, even if you didn't always take my advice about the decision you were about to make. I cheered your every triumph, and I was there to console you when things did not go your way. I laughed at your crazy jokes, and I cheered for you even when you failed.

"And you were there for me too. When life kicked me the hardest, you were the only one—the *only* one—who saw my tears when we received the news that my older brother, Jason, would not be coming home from Vietnam."

Burt's voice cracked as he silently whipped a tear from his right eye, as he talked about his brother, Jason.

"And how about the night we had to take Dad's car back home with a badly bent front fender after we hit a cow on that country road. It was all your fault, Twinkles, because I was looking at you instead of looking at that dark country road."

"Are you about finished?" Twinkles asked. "Anyway, time's up."

With a deep sense of failure, Burt slowly turned the key and started up the car. The powerful engine sprang to life.

Usually the very sound of those powerful horses coming to life under that hood would send a feeling of raging stallions rushing through his veins.

But tonight the only feelings running through this driver were defeat and failure.

"Give me a hug for good luck before you go," the man quietly requested.

Letting a half smile escape her lips, Twinkles slid back across the front seat to comply with his request and then prepared to leave.

It was almost like a scene from one of those old black-and-white movies…almost.

"Why? Why?" he asked himself. "Why must it always end like this?"

"It would have been so much easier to take her into my arms and give her the loving kiss that she doesn't even know she needs," Burt tried to counsel himself.

"And for what? Why am I always the one in second place? The one who is always there to patch up her latest romantic problem," he had told himself time and time again.

The possibility of losing again was just too hard to take.

Sadly, Burt began to accept the fact that this had been a great waste of time and effort.

"So much effort, for what? Maybe a break from Twinkles was not such a bad thing. Well, this time things will be different. No more trying to patch up Twinkles's broken affairs. If some guy dumps her or if she tires of her next lover boy, so be it. I have my own life to live," he told himself.

Meanwhile Twinkles was sitting on the wooden steps leading to the front porch. She was not ready to engage in family chitchat about her day. And she was sure that her father or mother would be sitting in the living room, waiting to ask her about her day.

So much had happened in Twinkles's life in the last twenty-four hours. First is the total breakup with Howard, then this unexpected sermon from Burt, especially coming from Burt.

She had never suspected—or even dreamed—that Burt would ever take sides against her. He had always been her "rock," the one that she could always depend on.

She looked up from her deep thoughts to see that Burt had quietly backed out of the family driveway and disappeared into the night.

"Burt!" she cried out. "Burt, where are you!"

CHAPTER 10

Howard's Last Harough

It was a chilly night in mid-October, and Twinkles was feeling bored.

She had just completed her notes for her oral presentation in class the following day on her least favorite topic: "Strategies for Advertising and Marketing, I."

Believing that her tireless efforts on this project had earned her a suitable reward, Twinkles decided that a nice glass of sparkling white wine would suit the occasion just fine.

Twinkles seldom drank alone, but with Alice at home nursing a headache, this self-confident young lady decided to do it alone for once.

Looking at her reflection in her full-length mirror, she decided that her black slacks and light blue blouse would be just fine. After all it was just for a glass of wine.

Grabbing a light jacket to shield her from the cool night air, and leaving her car behind, she chose to walk the short distance and enjoy the crisp night air.

Twinkles found the Drunken Horse Bar and Grill to be only lightly occupied on this Sunday evening.

After scanning the friendly pub, she settled for a seat at the unoccupied bar.

Hearing a familiar voice call her by name, Twinkles looked up to see Cliff Ellis smiling at her from behind the bar. She and Cliff had attended a business marketing class two years prior and had become friends but never became romantically involved.

This was because he was then engaged to another classmate, whom he eventually married.

"What a surprise!" Cliff exclaimed, with a big smile. "Back here for one more year of brain drain?"

"Of course," she replied. "My final year."

Changing the subject, Twinkles added, "How is Ellie?"

"Pregnant, I'm happy to say," he replied.

"Well, look at you," Twinkles replied with a big smile. "When is the happy date?"

"In three more months. We are looking forward to a blessed Christmas event."

"My word. You don't waste any time, do you?"

"And how about you, Twinkles? What do you have to say about your love life?" he asked with a sly grin.

"Oh, nothing new to report. I'm still the same old boring me," she replied.

Cocking his head to one side, her friend teased, "A little bird told me that you still get around."

"And what gossip have you been hearing?" she asked.

"It appears that you are more popular than you would have me believe," came the mysterious reply. "In fact, at this very moment, there is a handsome man-about-town who has been inquiring about you this very evening," Cliff replied.

"About me?" she asked in surprise. "I think you have me confused with someone else."

"Not a chance, young lady." Cliff came back with that same grin, "As a matter of fact, that gentleman is still here in this very bar."

Seeing that there was no other person at the bar seeking service, the smiling friend leaned close to Twinkles and said, "If you will give me a moment, I shall produce that person right now."

Still quite puzzled by this unexpected development, Twinkles sat and waited as Cliff stepped from behind the bar and approached a young man who was seated with his back facing the bar while conversing with another man.

Although Twinkles could see Cliff and the other man, she was not close enough to hear what was being said.

By now, Twinkles was totally confused by this stranger in the heavy coat, but that was all to be cleared up in a few seconds when the man stood up and turned around.

The mystery was immediately solved when Howard smiled at her.

"Well, fancy meeting you here, in a bar, and unescorted too. Can this be the same sweet lady I have been courting these last few months?"

"One and the same," she replied with a simple wave of her hand.

"What have you been up to lately?" Howard asked. "Haven't seen much of you since you started work on that oral presentation you have to present for Professor Hinkley."

"My presentation is tomorrow morning, and I just finished my final run-through this evening," she explained. "I figured that I deserved a glass of wine to help me relax before I rest."

"And wine helps you do that?" he calmly inquired. "Most women I know tend to get a little tipsy on wine."

Still keeping the conversation light while making her point, Twinkles replied, "I don't let myself get 'tipsy,' and I'm not like most other women."

"Pow!" the surprised young fellow replied, as he jolted back in his chair, as if he had been shot. "You don't pull your punches, do you?"

"No need to," she calmly replied. "If a person has something to say, then she should just come out and say it. It saves a lot of time and a lot of miscommunication."

"I like a woman who speaks her mind freely," the man said. "It cuts through a lot of chatter, so to speak."

"In that same vein, might I ask if you would like to join me in my hotel, where we could continue this pleasant conversation over another glass of less inferior wine?"

"Might you ask?" she answered his question with one of her own. "Of course, you may ask," she continued to play along. "But that does not mean that I will consent to your request. After all we are good friends, but not yet close friends."

"But it is only a glass of wine shared by two adults," he pointed out.

"In a hotel room, in the middle of the night," she came back as she placed $10 on the bar and nodded at Cliff before pitching up her bag and heading for the door.

"You don't have to leave," Howard shot back. "We can continue our conversation right here."

"That's all right. I need to get back. Tomorrow is Monday. I have things to prepare. I enjoyed the wine. See you around."

"Wait a minute," he called out to her back as she was walking away.

Then dropping his hand, he said to himself, "Oh, let her go."

CHAPTER 11

Plans Come Crashing Down

Alice leaned through the open window to give Freddy a quick kiss before Freddy slowly put the car into first gear and eased it into the center of the nearly deserted side street.

After a few shouted *goodbyes*, Alice returned to her home as the shiny car turned the corner at the end of the block and disappeared.

With her boyfriend's kiss still warm on her lips, Alice entered her house to tell her younger sister all about Burt's shiny car and how Freddy was allowed to drive it.

As the two Miller girls talked excitedly about Alice's boyfriend, Freddy was getting more familiar with the sporty machine.

"Let's take her down Main Street," Burt suggested. "It will give you a chance to show off a bit."

All the while, Burt was getting more confidence in his tall friend's handling of the car.

As was expected, there was greater traffic near the center of town, but Freddy was continuing to handle the car quite well.

Again, at Burt's suggestion, Freddy pulled into an open parking space near the Frozen Iglo, a popular ice cream shop in town.

Within minutes, a small group of high school and college students gathered around. This car was seldom seen on the streets of White Hill, Indiana.

"What are you up to tonight?" came a call from somewhere in the back of the crowd.

"Just cruising with my 'pride and joy,'" Burt replied easily.

"Don't put your hands on the car," came a warning from some-one near the back. "The sweat from your hands could damage the special paint."

"Not to worry," the proud car owner called out. "This baby has had two coats of fresh paint and then two more coats of protective sealer."

Finally a friendly voice in the crown asked, "Burt, why in the world would you bring a classy car like that to an ice cream joint?"

"To get some ice cream, of course," came the reply. "Now if you guys would step back a bit, we could get out and do just that."

Quickly moving to the only open table, the guys tried to attract a cute, but very busy, waitress.

Suddenly Freddy spotted his new friend, Shantelle, seated with a middle-aged man.

Freddy pointed out the presence of the new college transfer student and asked himself if he should go over to their table and say *hi*.

Burt, who had overheard Freddy's mumbling, advised against the idea, saying, "They seem to be engaged in a serious conversation. Best to leave them alone."

After finishing their frozen treats, Burt consented to let Freddy drive the car a little while longer.

It was getting late, and there was no other traffic on the streets, so Freddy decided to take the car to Hunters Hill on the outskirts of town.

While Freddy was gaining more self-confidence, Burt, on the other hand, was beginning to have some second thoughts about letting Freddy continue to test the limits of the high-performance car. Freddy was gaining more confidence with each passing moment.

When Freddy left the main road and turned onto Sandrill Road, Burt's concerns became real.

"Let's see just what this baby can do," Freddy said, as he hit the gas and headed up Sandhill Road.

Meanwhile, Burt was beginning to feel a sense of foreboding as they began to pick up speed as it climbed the hill with ease.

"Relax," Freddy replied. "I've been up this hill a hundred times, but never in a machine like this."

Burt was expiring real panic as they passed a 25 mph sign while going nearly 40.

"Slow down!" Burt ordered. "You know that there is a sharp turn up at the top. We are not going to make it!"

"This baby will do it just fine," replied the overconfident Freddy.

"Shut this thing down *now*," Burt barked in a voice that would put an Army drill sergeant to shame.

Freddy quickly turned the steering wheel and was able to slide through the turn successfully, but the car was now sliding sideways, straight for the old weatherworn guardrail.

The tragic, pending outcome of this ill-fated test drive was all too obvious to the two helpless men in the skidding classic car.

No final words were exchanged as time appeared to stand still as they watched in silence as the totally ineffective barrier drew closer and closer. Then came the blinding, unstoppable speed of the crashing descent to the silently waiting cow pasture below.

After the vehicle landed—upside down—the only sound to be heard was the spinning of the right front wheel, a lingering testimony to the end of one young man's dream and another young man's life.

Meanwhile, as Burt and Freddy were crashing to the bottom of White Hill, Twinkles was leisurely preparing for another restful night's rest. Dressed in her favorite light-green PVs and with a glass of slightly heated milk, she was the picture of tranquility.

Little did she suspect that her life was to change so drastically in the next few hours.

Getting out of bed for the fourth time to change the channel of her recently received twelve-inch black-and-white TV (Christmas gift from Mom and Dad), Twinkles finally decided that she was set for the night.

While waiting for the seemingly endless TV commercials, Twinkles's calm late evening was suddenly disrupted by the ringing of her private bedside phone.

Who could this be? she wondered. Especially on a Sunday night.

"Hello," she answered slowly, trying to make herself sound sleepier than she actually was. "Who is this?"

"Twinkles, are you watching the ten o'clock news?" Alice asked with almost panic in her voice.

"Of course not," the impatient friend replied. "I'm waiting for my favorite show to start. What's up?"

"There has been a terrible accident just outside of town."

"Is it someone we know?" a now serious Twinkles asked.

"They haven't released any names yet," Alice replied, almost in tears. "But they did say that the car was a black Charger."

"Daddy, come quick. I need you!" Twinkles dropped her phone and called out again.

Recognizing the pain in his daughter's voice, Mr. Booker literally bounded up the stairs to his daughter's room, with his wife close behind. As he entered her bedroom, he quickly dropped to one knee and asked, "Baby, what is the problem?"

"Daddy, there has been a terrible accident tonight out on Hunters Hill, and the report said that the car was a black Dodge Charger. There is only one of those here. Daddy, tell me that it was not Burt. Please, Daddy, tell me that it was not him."

It was an open secret in the Booker home that even at twenty-one, Twinkles was still "Daddy's girl." Of course, there would always be time for Mother's comforting, but for now, this was Daddy time.

"Is there someone you can call?" Twinkles's mother asked.

Being an ex–county sheriff, Mr. Booker still had friends on the "force" that he could contact now and again. "I'll give Jim a call. He might have some more recent information," the troubled father replied as he returned downstairs to his private office.

With her father's departure, Mrs. Booker took her husband's place beside her grieving daughter.

Twinkles's father reentered the young lady's bedroom.

"What new information did you learn?" Twinkles needed to know. "Tell me that it wasn't Burt."

"I can't tell you that, baby, because they just now turn the car right side up. They cannot release any names yet. All they could tell me was that the driver of the car did not survive. They are trying to get the surviving passenger out and to the hospital."

Twinkles's tears burst forth again, even stronger this time as she fell into her mother's wailing arms.

CHAPTER 12

Unexpected Visitors Drop In

Mr. Bradshaw was just finishing his bedtime snack of buttered toast and black coffee when he heard a loud crashing sound coming from the small cow pasture located behind his house.

Old Sam Bradshaw was a retired lifelong farmer, and when he gave up farming four years before due to failing health, he managed to find this small four-acre plot of ground at the base of Hunters Hill with a small house and a fenced area leading right up to the back side of the big local landmark.

The reason Old Sam wanted the fenced area was because he could not dare to part with his two favorite milk cows, Clara Bell and Rainbow.

It was more out of concern for his two bovine friends than anything else that caused him to grab his handy flashlight and hurry out his backdoor and into the small pasture.

After ensuring that his sources of good, fresh farm-grade milk were unaffected by whatever made such a loud commotion at this late hour, Old Man Bradshaw turned his attention to finding the source of that late-night disturbance.

The cautious retired farmer used his flashlight more on the ground in front of him (trying to avoid possible cow patties). Soon he was forced to stop because he was about to walk directly into an overturned automobile.

Although there was no fire present, there was some smoke coming from the wreckage.

Upon shining his light into the vehicle, Sam could identify two motionless human bodies.

Turning around to face his house, he immediately called out to his wife, "Ethel, call 911 right now! We need help, quickly. We have a wreck in our backyard!"

As Sam entered the house, his hapless wife was still fumbling with the phone book, trying to find the emergency phone number.

Taking the phone from his wife, he quickly dialed 911.

The young lady at the other end of the line politely answered the emergency call with "911, what is your emergency?"

"I have an upside-down car in my backyard!"

"This is an emergency line. You need to call a wrecking company," came the immediate advice.

When the emergency operator hung up the phone and turned to her only other officemate, she remarked, "That's the problem with this midnight shift. You get all these crazies."

"One night I had this group of kids call in and ask me to call the fire department because their chilly was too hot."

"There ought to be a law against calls like that," her coworker commented.

She would have told her coworker more, but the 911 line lit up again.

"911, what is your emergency" the lady calmly answered.

"Hey, lady! Don't hang up on me again! This is a real emergency!"

"I know," came the calm reply. "Someone parked his car in your backyard. We get this call all the time."

"And they parked it upside down," her friend chimed in.

"This is no joke, lady. I live at the back of Hunters Hill, and a car crashed through that guardrail and ended up in my backyard. There are people inside, and we need help here! Right now!"

"Yes, sir," the operator quickly responded. "Give me your address, and we'll have help there right away. My assistant is on the phone with the police and fire department right now. Please stay on the line in case we need more information."

CHAPTER 13

Confrontation

The angry middle-aged man walked quickly into the hospital waiting room. Mr. Hank Willkerson was a tall man with early graying hair and steely gray eyes. His eyes grew more intense as his emotions grew stronger; and this day, at 6:35 a.m., those eyes were vividly ablaze with emotion.

A young hospital attendant noticed the man's agitated state and approached him, asking if there was something that she could do for him.

"I'm looking for Mr. Nickels. I understand that he is here."

"That's right," came the polite response from the young lady. "He is in with his wife in a private waiting room. His son was in a vehicle accident last night, and I don't think that he and his wife can be disturbed right now."

"Well, he is going to be more disturbed when I get through with him."

"I can't let you go in there, but if you will tell me your name, I'll see if he can come out here for a few minutes."

"Just tell him that Freddy's dad wants to talk to him. Now!"

Slightly shaken by the man's sudden outburst, the medical attendant hurried off to deliver the urgent message.

Sensing the urgency of the situation, John Nickels hurried to the main waiting room to talk with Freddy's dad.

"Hank," Mr. Nickels started, reaching out his hand.

Ignoring the offered handshake, Mr. Willkerson accused, "It's that son of yours that has brought on all this grief. I knew that that fancy high-powered machine would lead to no good someday."

"But wait a minute, Hank," John tried to reply.

But Mr. Willkerson cut him off in midsentence. "I've seen your son running around town and showing off that racey sports car. I knew that it was only a matter of time until he got somebody killed with that thing. Now it has finally happened."

"Hold on, Hank," Mr. Nickels broke in, more determined this time.

"You think that Burt was driving that car?"

"Who else," Hank roared back.

"Your son was behind the wheel of that car at the time of the crash. Didn't the police tell you that?"

"Are you sure about that?" the grieving man asked.

"Of course, didn't they tell you that?"

"No. All they said was that my son didn't make it and that your son was here at the hospital. Are you sure?" Mr. Willkerson asked again.

"Yes, I'm sure," Mr. Nickels reaffirmed. "If you want to hear it for yourself, call the sheriff's department and ask for Sgt. Kelly. He was first on the scene last night."

Hank Willkerson fell silent as he turned around and dropped into a nearby chair.

"My son told me that Freddy had been begging him to let him drive the Charger for over two months. I guess he finally gave in and handed him the keys."

Feeling spent and totally exhausted, Mr. Willkerson got up and silently walked out the door.

CHAPTER 14

Good and Bad Discoveries

It was shortly after midnight in the Booker house, yet all four members of the family were still sitting in the home's living room, awaiting any further developments on the tragic car accident out on Hunters Hill just hours before.

Jenna, Twinkles's younger sister, was seated nearest to the telephone when that instrument suddenly broke that silence with its long-awaited ring.

Quickly Jenna answered the call, saying, "Booker residence."

After a short silence, the teen said, "Mr. Booker? Yes, he is here. Who shall I say is calling?"

"It's for you, Dad," she relayed. "It is a Sgt. Kelly."

"I'll take it in my office. Be sure to hang up the phone as soon as you hear my voice on the line."

Mr. Booker quickly moved to his office and picked up his extension phone and told his daughter to hang up.

Whatever Sgt. Kelly had to say, Mr. Booker wanted to be the first to hear it, before relaying it to the rest of the family.

Holding the phone close to his ear, he quietly asked, "Is that you, Jim? Do you have any further information for me?"

"Yes. We know that both men were in the front seat of the car at the time of the crash," Sgt. Kelly relayed.

"We know all that. Tell me something we don't know."

"This information is new. We have identified the driver of the car, and it is not who you think it was."

"The authorities are positive now that it was Freddy Willkerson who was driving at the time of the accident."

"Our officers are making personal notification to the Willkerson family as we speak. I thought you would like to know so that you could tell your daughter the information straight from you and not from some morning newscaster."

"Thanks, Jim. I owe you one," Mr. Booker said.

Hanging up the phone, Mr. Booker called all his family to come join him in his office, immediately.

"Twinkles, come here," Mr. Booker said, "because this latest news affects you the most."

"Daddy, please don't give me any more bad news. I can't take any more."

"For you, this is the best possible news."

"Please, Daddy, tell me."

"The driver of that car last night was not Burt. He is now safe in the hospital, undergoing emergency surgery. His injuries are serious, but not life-threatening."

Immediately Twinkles hugged her dad. Tears were freely flowing from everyone in the small room.

"Is it really true?" Twinkles asked. She had to be sure.

Suddenly Twinkles sat up straight and called out, "Freddy!"

"That's right," Mr. Booker confirmed. "The driver of the car at the time of the accident was Freddy."

"Burt must have given in to Freddy's many requests and let Freddy drive the car."

"The problem was that Freddy drove it up Sandstone Drive too fast and was unable to make the sharp turn at the top of that hill."

"They crashed through that old guardrail and rolled down the back side of that hill and ended up in a small cow pasture below. The car ended up on its roof."

Initially everyone assumed that since it was Burt's car, the driver of the car was most likely Burt.

"That is why the sheriff's office did not officially identify the lone fatality by name until much later."

Suddenly Twinkles remembered her dear friend and called out, "Alice! She must know by now."

"Maybe not," Mr. Booker offered. "The sheriff's office will need to notify the Willkerson family first. Alice is not a member of that family, so there will be no direct notification there."

"Shall I call her, Daddy?" Twinkles wanted to be right.

"I would say not," her father advised. "Let Alice's family comfort her tonight."

"Well, I know where I'm going," Twinkles announced. "I'm headed for the hospital."

"You can't go there at this hour," her mother advised. "They will never let you in."

"I'll go straight to the emergency room. They never close," Twinkles called out as she headed for the door.

CHAPTER 15

Shantelle Gets Shocked Awake

S hantelle had just poured herself a glass of fresh squished orange juice. She then picked up the morning paper from just outside the door of her second-floor apartment.

Turning the currently upside-down newspaper to its normal position, the slow-moving young lady was suddenly shocked wide awake by the bold black-and-white headline: PROMISING LOCAL NBA PROSPECT DEAD AT 21.

Shantelle could think of only one person in Hillside who could match that description: Freddy Willkerson.

Dropping the unread newspaper on the floor before her, Shantelle grabbed the TV clicker and selected the Sunday morning TV news.

Quite by accident, the distressed young lady caught the Indianapolis TV station just beginning its coverage of last night's accident.

"Late last night, the neighboring town of White Hill, Indiana, lost its promising NBA prospect when Freddy Willkerson perished in a one-car accident on Hunters Hill, just outside the small upstate town.

"Details of the crash are still sketchy at this time, but it has been confirmed that a lone passenger in the car at the time of the accident, a Mr. Burtrom 'Burt' Nickels, survived. Mr. Nickels is currently receiving treatment at White Hill General Hospital, with non-life-threatening injuries."

"Several NBA teams have made no secret that they were interested in courting the promising college basketball forward, who shocked the basketball world with his outstanding performance in that team's stunning upset win over the Indianapolis Titans."

"We will continue to update this story as more details become available."

"Meanwhile the NBA is still in shock over the untimely passing of Freddy Willkerson."

Of all the people Shantelle knew in this small town, the one most likely to know the latest details would be Twinkles.

When Shantelle first heard Twinkles's familiar voice, she assumed that her friend was at home.

She was somewhat surprised to learn that Twinkles was still at the local hospital.

"Are you still there?" Shantelle asked in surprise.

Yes was Twinkles's sleepy answer. "The night nurse let me sleep in a chair while I waited for Burt to get out of surgery. And then once he was here in his room, I couldn't just walk out and leave him here."

"Weren't any of his family there?" her friend asked.

"Yes, of course," Twinkles answered. "But Burt kept asking for me, and his mother asked me if I could stay with them for a while."

"How is he?" Shantelle asked. "Will his injuries be permanent?"

"The surgeon who spoke to the family said that it was too early to tell completely but did let them know that there probably would be some permanent damage. He said that they would know more by tomorrow."

"Twinkles, you sound like a wreck," Shantelle said. "And I don't mean that as an insult. You need to get some rest for yourself."

"That's all right," Twinkles came back. "I couldn't rest if I went home anyway. Mrs. Nickels said that I could stay as long as I wanted. Burt still keeps asking for me."

"Have you heard anything from Alice?" Shantelle inquired quite seriously. "She must be devastated."

"I tried to talk to her, but she was very angry, and she wouldn't talk to me. It was like she was blaming me for Freddy's accident."

"When we first got the report of the accident, everyone, including me, thought that the one fatality was Burt because the police said that the only fatality was the driver. You know Burt," she explained. "Burt had never let anyone drive his car, so we put two and two together and got five." No one knew that Burt had finally agreed to let Freddy drive.

It wasn't until the car was turned right side up that the police realized that the driver was Freddy.

"That must have been terrible for you to falsely believe that Burt was the one," Shantelle imagined.

"It was," Twinkles admitted. "I couldn't let myself accept that news. I even asked my dad over and over if he was sure. I prayed so hard that the report was wrong, and in the end, it did turn out to be wrong."

"But in that time when we all thought that it was actually Burt, Alice was there for me and even prayed with me. But then she found out—when we all found out—that the one was actually Freddy, she flipped. She could not accept the news, just like I could not accept it when the first, unofficial, word was wrong."

Changing the subject to lighten things up a bit, Shantelle offered, "Can I bring you anything to eat? A hot dog, a pizza, a cold beer?" That last suggestion brought forth a hearty cheer.

"Now that you mention it," Twinkles replied, "they have some deli sandwiches in the vending machine in the waiting room."

"Not a chance, kid," Shantelle shot back. "I've eaten vending machine food before. There is a deli across the street from the hospital. I'll get you some real food."

Before hanging up, Shantelle asked Twinkles to see if Mrs. Willkerson would like something also.

Twinkles relayed Shantelle's offer, which she kindly declined, explaining that her husband would be arriving shortly to relieve her and that she would get something at her home.

After arriving with the requested food, the two young ladies and Mrs. Nickels sat and chatted for several minutes until Mr. Nickels arrived to wait with Twinkles while Mrs. Nickels took her turn getting some much-needed rest.

CHAPTER 16

Stop That Man

"Stop that man!" Twinkles called out, as she followed a young man through the main hallway of the administration building. Second-semester registration was in full swing for early January 1977.

Stepping from behind his raised security desk in the administration building, Security Officer Gordon called for the young lady and the man she was chasing to come to a stop before him.

"Just what is the cause for this commotion this fine morning?" he politely asked, speaking first to the young lady.

"He tried to kill me, Officer," she cried out.

"Right here? This morning?" the officer inquired.

"No. Not now. It was on the first day of registration, last fall," she tried to clarify.

"One moment, young lady. Before we go any further, may I know your name?"

"Of course," she quickly replied. "My name is Terry Booker, and I am a student here."

"Officer," the young man broke in, "I have no idea of what she is talking about."

"Just be patient for a moment," the officer advised. "When I finish with this young lady, I'll give you a chance to tell me what happened."

"But, officer, I have never seen this crazy lady before," the impatient man continued.

"I asked you to wait," the officer reminded the man. "You will have your chance to tell your side of things in just a few moments."

Then turning back to Twinkles, he asked, "What kind of weapon did he use for this alleged assault? A knife? A gun?"

"No, Officer," the lady cut in. "It was with his car."

"You mean he tried to run you down with his car?" Officer Gordon asked as he tried to keep a straight face.

By now a small crowd had gathered in the hallway.

"And this all happened five months ago? Then why did you wait so long to report it, Ms. Booker?"

"Today is the first time that I have seen this man since the accident. No, not really an accident. I was quick enough to slam on my brakes," she reported.

"Now," turning to the now patient young man, Officer Gordon asked, "May I have your name, please?"

"Yes, Officer," came the quick reply. "My name is Jeffery Watts, and I am a new student here."

"All right, Mr. Watts, what say you in your defense?"

"Plenty, Officer," came his quick reply. "I now think I know what the young lady is referring to, and I can clear it up quickly."

"I hope so," the officer remarked with a sigh. "I was getting ready to turn you both over to the county sheriff's office.

"It all happened on registration day last fall, just as she said. It was my first day in this town, and I was looking for street signs and not concentrating on stop lights. I admit that that was a mistake on my part, and I apologize for that. But it was not intentional nor malicious. I admit that it was my fault, and I apologize for it."

"Sir, your explanation appears logical and forgivable," the officer said, "but I believe that you gave it to the wrong person. I think that if you were to give that same apology to that young lady here, and maybe with a cappuccino, you will both feel much better."

Turning to Twinkles, Jeffery repeated his apology and added, "How about that cappuccino? We should follow the kind officer's advice, or was that an official order? I think we should have our special coffee and talk and get to know each other."

As the two students entered the cafeteria and ordered their java, Officer Gordon was shaking his head and mumbling to himself, "This is one report that will never make its way into the official logbook."

"I don't normally drink with strangers. At least not this early in the day," Twinkles confessed. "But I think that I can make an exception, just once."

Secretly, to herself, Twinkles had to admit that, up close, this guy was really not that bad-looking.

CHAPTER 17

Come See My Texas

As Twinkles entered the crowded college cafeteria, she was pleasantly surprised to find her new friend, Jeffery, already seated at a small corner table.

Using her best "damsel in distress" smile, Twinkles approached the young man's table and asked, "Is this seat taken?"

"It is waiting for you," he replied as he rose to offer the seat to her. "What brings you out so early?"

"It's a Monday, you know," she replied. "There might be traffic."

"Traffic?" Jeffery said in surprise. "You, people, don't even know what traffic is like until you sit at the same traffic light for three minutes, waiting for your turn to proceed. I'll bet the only traffic you see in this town is the annual Fourth of July parade."

"Well, there is at least one advantage we have over Las Vegas," Twinkles shot back.

"What could that possibly be?" Jeffery inquired.

"We don't have traffic jams."

"I give up," her new friend replied as he playfully threw his hands up. "You are just too sharp for me. Seriously?" Jeffery asked. "You have never been to Texas before?"

"Scout's honor," came the quick reply.

"And I'll bet you were a cute little Girl Scout cookie salesgirl."

"What is Texas like?" Twinkles asked, getting more serious.

"It's like," Jeffery started. Then he stopped and began again, "It is just too big to explain. You have to see it for yourself—to experience it. Let me take you there on spring break," he offered.

"Are you serious?" Twinkles asked with a big smile.

"Very serious, and you need to get away."

Although Twinkles was inwardly grieving the loss of her dear friend, Freddy, she decided to accept this offer and try to move on, with Jeffery's help.

This flight just might help her ease some of the pain.

"Well," she said to herself, "you must realize that in small-town India, in 1977, one does not just jump on a plane, especially on a *jet*, and fly all the way to Texas."

*****

Three weeks later…

Naturally Twinkles insisted on getting the window seat so she could see America from above.

Jeffery was quite content to take the aisle seat and watch the stewardesses walk up and down the aisle.

Another surprise awaited the pretty traveler once they had arrived at the San Antonio terminal.

Twinkles had expected that Jeffery would make an effort to call a taxi for them, but he just stood calmly waiting.

After no more than a minute, her concerns were eased when Jeffery raised his hand and a neatly uniformed gentleman appeared and proceeded to pick up all four pieces of their luggage and took them to a waiting Mercedes.

Instantly the polite gentleman loaded the parcels into the car and returned to the waiting passengers.

When the surprised young lady reached to open the car door, Jeffery quickly reached out and took hold of her hand and pulled it back.

Without a word, or smile, the white-gloved hand of the driver reached out and quickly opened the car door and, as quickly, stepped back to allow Twinkles to enter the car.

Once all passengers were seated and secured, the highly efficient chauffeur maneuvered the car through the airport traffic and onto the main road for the twenty-minute drive to the Watts Ranch.

As they entered the Ranch House grounds, Twinkles noticed the driver key his radio and speak into it.

Twinkles was unable to hear the conversation, but she was convinced that it had something to do with their arrival. The efficient driver quickly assisted his passengers to a quick and safe exit and then drove away.

At this point, a small group of greeters moved to a position directly in front of the impressive building.

As the lady at the front of the group stepped forward, Jeffery left Twinkles's side and turned to face Twinkles, saying, "Twinkles, this is my mother, affectionately known in these parts as *Mama Sandy*."

Then, turning to his mother, he proudly stated, "Mother, this is Terry 'Twinkles' Booker. She is my classmate at Indiana Normal College, and she is finishing up her final semester for her degree in journalism, and she is as pretty as a Texas rose."

"Well, welcome to Watts Ranch, Miss Twinkles. Hope you had a pleasant flight from somewhere north of the Mason–Dixon Line, and if there is anything that you desire during your stay here, you just let Mama Sandy know, and I'll send Jeffery out to get it. Now come on inside and see how great Texas Ranch House looks like."

CHAPTER 18

Twinkles Gets the Guided Tour

Randolf, the Watts family chauffeur, just returned from taking the Watts family and their special house guest to Sunday religious services when he received a call from Mama Sandy. She simply informed him that she had a driving task for him, and she would like to have the Mercedes at the front door in ten minutes. She also requested that he come into the house to receive some special instruction for the afternoon use of her Mercedes.

When Randolf arrived at the house, he was surprised that Auntie Sandy was not going to go along on this unspecified trip. This was doubly unusual because, wherever that car went, Auntie Sandy was always seated in the right rear seat. She never rode in the left rear seat because Randolf's big head blocked her view.

The driver's concerns were quickly dispelled when she explained that for this trip only, her son, Jeffery, would be in charge of the car and its destinations, "If they were not illegal," she added with a chuckle.

This is Jeffery's chance to show his *little* girl all around San Antonio. Aunt Sandy just could not pass up a chance to tease the small girl from Indiana.

The mostly lonely ranch owner usually had little opportunity to experience true humor while presenting an iron-fist approach when in front of her ranch hands.

As if on cue, Jeffery and Twinkles entered Mother's office, where their driver stood waiting.

As the trio turned to leave, Mama advised her son, "If there is anything that you want or need, like food, souvenirs, entrance fees somewhere, Randolf has an allotment of cash to take care of your expenses."

"That won't be necessary, Mother," Jeffery quickly replied. "I came prepared for this trip, but thanks anyway. I appreciate the offer."

As Mama Sandy watched the trio leave the room and head for her car, Mama whispered to herself, "It looks like the young boy is beginning to take some responsibility for his decisions. I wonder if this new love interest has had any influence in that?"

In a matter of minutes, the happy couple and their stone-faced driver were on their way.

"Where to first, Mr. Jeffery?" the driver inquired.

"Let's start at the Alamo," Jeffery decided. "A little history is a good place to start."

"Is this going to be a history lesson?" Twinkles joked.

"Actually, yes. This is probably one of the most famous events in Texas history.

Within minutes, the couple's silent driver pulled into an open parking space. As expected, Randolf remained with the vehicle.

*****

Viewing the plain-looking building for the first time, Twinkles asked, "Why is this building so special?"

"Because," Jeffery explained, "in the mid-1860s, a small group of American soldiers were occupying the Alamo, and Mexico claimed it as their own.

Colonel Travis was ordered to gather a group of volunteers and go to the Alamo and defend it.

Travis told these men that they may not live to see their loved ones again. Despite these odds, not one of the volunteers took that offer to leave.

"After fighting the enemy for thirteen straight days, and running out of ammunition, the small band of defenders were overrun and killed—every one."

"You mean they all died?" she asked with teary eyes. "I don't think I want to see any more of your monuments."

"I'm sorry, Twinkles. I didn't mean to make you so sad."

Then changing the subject to something more fun, Jeffery offered, "I know a place that is guaranteed to make you laugh.

"I sure hope so," the young lady replied.

"This place is only a very short walk," he told her.

Within minutes, the pair arrived at a local park where a traveling carnival had set up its colorful rides and attractions.

Jeffery was pleased to see that his favorite stan was still with the group. It was Amazing Marshan and his fantastic future forecasts. (What other kind of forecast could there be?)

A handwritten sign also read: "Accurate 15%."

Jeffery smiled at his favorite yearly visitor and proudly introduced Twinkles.

With a thoughtful look and a tug on his long white beard, Marshan declared, "Twinkles? With a name like that, you should be in a carnival."

"Thanks, but no thanks," Twinkles quickly replied. "I'm doing quite well where I am."

"I'll bet you are," he replied with a sideways wink to Jeffery.

"Now what sports questions can I answer for you today?"

"First of all," Jeffery inquired, "just how much is your knowledge worth?"

"Actually thousands, but for you today only, I can go for a buck a 'pop.'"

Placing a crisp "ten" on the counter and turning to his friend, he encouraged, "Ask away."

"First of all, I am not a wizard. I am an ordinary person who can see things that other people cannot see."

"I'll give you ten-to-one odds on that statement," Jeffery remarked, as he looked at Twinkles and nodded his head at Marshan.

"Can you tell me if San Antonio will ever have a professional basketball team?" Twinkles inquired.

"Not only will they have a pro team, they will eventually win an NBA championship."

"You can't be serious?" Twinkles exclaimed.

"Hey, with a winning average of 15%, I have to be right at least once in a while," he rationalized.

"Well, Mr. Amazing," Twinkles ventured, "let me ask you one more question."

"Give it your best shot," he shot back.

"Will the Chicago White Sox ever win the World Series again?"

The sad-faced man answered her complex question with five simple words: "You should live so long."

After a few more of these pointless questions, Jeffery concluded that it was time to bid a friendly farewell to his traveling friend.

Turning to Twinkles, he asked if there was anything else on her list of sites to see.

Twinkle mentioned that one of her classmates at INC had once lived in San Antonio, and she told Twinkles to be sure to visit the beautiful River Walk.

"Excellent choice," Jeffery agreed. "They have boat rides in small gondolas on a quaint river which is flanked on both sides with cafés and restaurants on each side with refreshments and continuous lively music."

After another hour and a half, Jeffery asked his dazzled girlfriend if she was getting tired of all the walking and souvenir shopping.

Tinkles admitted that she was ready for a break and something cold to drink.

Jefferey quickly guided the happy pair to a brightly decorated sidewalk café and bar which he knew well and where the management knew him also.

Within minutes, a smiling jovial Mexican gentleman appeared to Jeffery, smiled, and then immediately asked about his attractive companion.

"Senior, you have been traveling in faraway places, my friend. We don't grow such light-skinned beauties this far south of Dallas."

"This is Hernando," Jeffery broke in. "He owns this local watering home."

"No need to ask what you are drinking. Your special is always at the ready. And for the lady, I have a special sweet wine specially aged for a thirsty young woman such as you."

"Should I?" Twinkles asked Jeffery. "It is midday."

"I remind you again," Jeffery teased her. "This is Texas, and we do things differently down here. Just relax and enjoy yourself."

"Words well-spoken," Hernando conquered.

After enjoying another half hour of this good-natured banter, Jeffery suggested that it was about time to return to the Mercedes and the ever-patient driver.

As the happy pair headed back to the Watts Ranch, Twinkles let herself slip into a comfortable, relaxed state, far from the recent disaster on Hunters Hill. This short trip with Jefferey had been a good idea.

She was beginning to be more patient and concerned about her lingering period of grieving over the loss of her friend. This trip had broken that sadness and returned a smiling Twinkles.

"Maybe my future is getting brighter," she said to herself.

CHAPTER 19

Mother's Council

All of Mama Sandy's regular guests were well aware that no one picked up a spoon or a salad fork until Mama had her "say," and tonight was no exception.

First of all, the beloved hostess acknowledged the presence of the special lady seated next to her son, Jeffery.

"Twinkles—I love that name—is my son's classmate at Indiana Normal College, where she is in her final semester of earning a degree in journalism."

"You should all be very thankful for her presence here tonight, because if it were not for this lady's presence, there would be no fancy dinner here this evening."

This announcement produced a unanimous round of cheering and hand clapping.

All present joined in the happy tribute to the young lady, except Twinkles herself, who appeared to be slightly embarrassed by all the unexpected attention.

Turning to face her husband, who was seated by her side, Mama Sandy introduced the one man in the room who needed no introduction by simply saying, "I give you the Man."

Rising slowly to his feet like a man preparing to accept his party's presidential nomination, the Man told the private gathering: "Jeffery has introduced into this house a fine young woman, a woman who has stolen my son's heart. She is also someone who we trust will be welcomed into your homes as well, with true Texas hospitality."

Then in an aside to his friends, he added, "Even if she is a Yankee."

A round of good-natured laughter greeted his last remark.

"My only other bit of information this evening is about an item I had entered into yesterday's official board meeting record, which stipulated that at the successful completion of his master's degree studies at Purdue University, Jeffery Watts will be offered a junior position on the corporation's board of directors."

As opposed to the previous announcement about his son's latest girlfriend, this announcement led to a rousing standing round of applause.

Once again, "Daddy" had managed to "steal the moment" right out from under his son's nose—in public.

With formalities over, the serving staff quickly set to work, serving the expertly prepared meal.

To add to this festive occasion, a three-piece musical group with an accompanying female vocalist quietly took their place to provide soothing dinner music—that is after a rousing rendition of "The Yellow Rose of Texas."

The happy gathering was treated to a wide variety of soft background music to the delight of all until the group's female singer announced a special song especially for the night's honored guest.

With all the dignity and poise of a ten-piece band, the little group offered eight bars of "intro" and then broke into an upbeat version of "Back Home Again in Indiana."

The surprise musical number brought down the house—so to speak—as everyone joined in on the chorus.

Meanwhile Twinkles was blushing and trying to make herself inconspicuous, all to no avail, with repeated calls for the young lady to say a few words and at Jeffery's urging remark, "You're in Texas now. You need to speak up."

Slowly Twinkles managed to stand up and turn to face the small ground.

Controlling her urge to run and hide, and calling on her past public speaking experience at her church group back in Indiana, she managed to say, "I am so happy to be here in Texas, for my very first time. The people are so friendly and open here. I guess that is why I got attracted to Jeffery here."

A few whistles and "yeehaws" were heard along with some good natural laughter.

"Mama Sandy has just treated me like family since the time I arrived. I know that I haven't been here long, but I can tell you this. This might be my first visit to Texas, but I'm sure it won't be my last."

Amid shouts and laughter, even the Man reached over to Twinkles and offered his hand, saying, "Welcome to Texas."

Later when the meal was over and the family and friends scattered to chat and swap stories, Mama Sandy silently entered the large living room, seeking her younger son.

Quickly she approached him and told him to follow her.

Seeing that his attractive lady friend was engaged in pleasant conversation with other ladies, Jeffery quickly followed his mother.

"What is it, Mother?" the young man inquired casually.

"It concerns you and that young lady out there," his mother replied.

"Is there something about her that you don't like?"

"On the contrary, son," she assured him. "In fact I find her to be very well-spoken and equally well-mannered. The problem, if there is one, is with you."

"What do you mean, Mama?" he quietly asked.

"I am quite sure that you know exactly what I mean," she quickly replied.

"Mama, you can't mean my medical problem?" the nervous young man asked.

"Just answer this one question. Have you told her about it?"

"Mama, that is such a personal matter, and there will be time enough in the coming weeks for me to handle that problem tactfully," he reassured.

"That is not good enough, son," she declared. "That is a fine woman that you brought here. She seems to have strong feelings for you. She deserved to know the truth and know it before you two go too far. The longer you wait, the harder it will be, for each of you. Did I make myself clear, son?"

"Yes, Mother. But, please, not on our vacation, not here. Let the two of us go back to the college, and I swear to you that I will tell her the truth. Mama, I give you my word. I will do as you say."

Reluctantly Mama Sandy relented and extended her hand to her son to shake on the agreement. "Remember, son, your word is your bond." Then, just before releasing his hand, she added one more condition.

"Of course, Mama, just name it," he readily agreed.

"Once you tell her, in person, call me and tell me how she took the news. Her reaction can tell you a lot about her character."

"You have my word, Mother," he quickly agreed.

Without saying another word, Jeffery got up and followed his mother out of the room and returned to Twinkles's side.

After various members of the evening's gathering started saying their farewells and leaving the memorable evening behind, Mama Sandy excused herself from the remaining guests and walked up the curved staircase to the second-floor bedroom area.

With Twinkles and Victoria close behind, Mama paused before a waiting bedroom and turned to address her smiling guest, saying, "Twinkles, this will be your room for the duration of your stay with us. Then motioning to the nervous young house girl standing beside Twinkles, she continued. "Victoria, here, will tend to your needs then retire to her area in a room next to yours, where she will be available if you should need anything during the night. I am not saying that you should retire now," the gracious hostess explained, "I'm just showing you your accommodations, and then you are free to rejoin that noisy crowd downstairs. Most of the ladies have been sent home with their drivers who will return for the men when they get tired of 'shoot the bull' and having their 'shots' of fine bourbon. It's a local tradition. And I imagine that you may be somewhat tired after your flight. So feel free to retire at any time you choose. We don't stand on ceremony here. These guys don't all get together that often, so that [pointing to the stairs] could go on for hours. After all this is Texas.

"Sleep well, and I trust that you will have a pleasant night's rest, and again, thank you for visiting our home."

"It is I who should be thanking you for your hospitality, and I do sincerely," Twinkles replied.

Pausing at the door, Mama added, "Sleep well, and remember breakfast is at 6:00 a.m., sharp!"

Sandy smiled to herself as she returned to the lower level to bid farewell to her few remaining lady guests before returning upstairs to her private quarters.

CHAPTER 20

Jeffery Drops a "Bomb"

"Today is a special day," Twinkles calmly announced.

When Jeff declined to ask why, Twink calmly asked, "Do you want to know why today is such a special day?"

"Sure. What makes today so special?" he replied, deciding to play along with her silly word game.

"Today marks two months that we have been together, and I think I'm beginning to like it."

"Now that is a news flash," Jeff came back. "What part of that is so surprising: the fact that it has lasted so long or the idea that you think you are just beginning to like it?"

"Both, silly," she replied with a warm smile. "Actually if you ask the girls around here that really know me, they will tell you that two months is close to being a record for me. And you have helped me break that record."

"And why is that?" Jeff came back with a puzzled look on his face.

"Honestly I don't know," she replied. "It seems like everything is going along fine, and then one day, it all falls apart. Maybe you are my lucky charm, and you have broken this evil spell."

"Well, since we are both being so honest this morning," Jeff spoke with a more serious tone. "Before we go on any further, there is one thing about me that it is only fair that I tell you now."

"Please, don't tell me that you have a terminal disease. That is about the only thing that I haven't been told," she quipped.

"It's not that, but it is serious, and I should have told you earlier, except—like you—I was waiting to see if this thing between us was going to work out. Now that things between us are starting to get serious, I feel that I have to tell you."

"Okay," Twinkles answered seriously. "You can tell me."

"First of all," he started, "I do not have terminal cancer. What I do have is just as serious, but not life-ending, which means that I could live a long time, but we could not have children together."

Twinkles fell silent for a few moments. This was something completely out of left field.

"Jeff is such a strong and active man. How could this be?" she asked herself.

"You have checked with the medical people, I'm sure," spoken more as a question than a statement.

"Of course," he replied. "I've seen some of the best."

"But medical doctors and specialists are always coming up with new treatments every day," she offered. "Is there anything that you can be?" Twinkles asked.

"Not for this," Jeff concluded.

"Then it's hopeless," the suddenly saddened lady said, mostly to herself.

"I know that this is not something that you'd want to hear," he started to explain. I didn't want to surprise you…

But before he could continue, Twinkles cut in.

"Surprise!" the lady mocked. "More like shocked! When were you planning to tell me about this great surprise? On the night of our wedding?"

"You have to understand. This is not something that you discuss on a first date."

"Well, if it is not, then it certainly should be," Twinkles shot back. "I just can't believe that you could go on deceiving me."

"Remember, Twinkles, this is 1977, and science is coming up with new treatments every day. I know that this must be a surprise to you," he started to reply.

"And then maybe in twenty years, I'll be middle-aged and childless. I don't like the odds. I think I'd better go," Twinkles concluded.

"Wait," Jeffery called out as the young lady started to leave. "It's the least I can do."

"No, not really," she mocked. "You have already done that."

As she left and headed for the street, where she could hail a cab, she called back over her shoulder, "At least my batting average is still intact. No runs, no hits, nothing but errors."

CHAPTER 21

Twinkles Seeks Friendly Advice

Twinkles Booker sat down uneasily in a soft, comfortable easy chair as Alice Miller handed her unexpected guest a glass of apple juice and asked the obvious question, "Well, Twinkles, what brings you here at this hour?" She pointed to the nearby wall clock, which registered a time of 10:15 p.m. "It seems a little odd that you would come to me after the way I rejected your help when you tried to comfort me when I got the news about Freddy," Alice explained.

"Twinkles, tell me what's up," Alice continued. "I can understand what you were going through back then, but how can I help you now?" Alice asked with genuine concern in her voice.

"It's about me, or maybe Burt. Then maybe it's about the two of us," the confused friend confessed. "I'm kinda mixed up, and I just need someone I can talk to, someone I can trust."

"It's about time," Alice explained with obvious relief. "You don't know how many years your friends have been waiting for this day," she continued.

"It's not like that," Twinkles quickly cut in. "At least I don't think so."

"So tell me, what happened?" Alice asked, now showing more concern.

"I slapped his face," the confused girl admitted. "He kissed me!"

"You what?" Alice asked in disbelief.

"I slapped him," Twinkles repeated. "I was shocked," she tried to explain.

"After all those years?" Alice asked in disbelief. "You two have been locked at the hip since high school. Why was this such a shock?"

"I know that everyone thinks that we look like the perfect couple, but we have been too close. And there was Howard last year. He was so continental, always knowing what I wanted, and how to please me, and always being the perfect gentleman."

"So what was wrong with that? Sounds like the perfect guy," Alice noted. "Never did understand that breakup."

"He was a great catch, except for one thing," the troubled young lady replied.

"He was impotent?" Alice guessed.

"No, silly," came the quick reply.

"What then?" her friend had to know.

"Howard, along with all his good points, has one trait that I could not stand."

"Quick, tell me."

"He is a control freak," she confessed. "He simply had to be in control of everything I did. He wanted to turn me into the perfect executive's wife. There was little time for fun in his world, at least not until he has established himself as a success in his father's eyes. It was nice for about two months, and then I gradually realized that I could not live the rest of my life like that," she explained.

"Moving on," Alice remarked. "Then this year, there was Jefferey, wasn't there?"

"Jeffery was nice, too, but he also had one fatal flaw."

"And what was that?" Alice was beginning to sound a little frustrated.

"Jeffery really is impotent," Twinkles sheepishly admitted.

"I'll say one thing for you," Alice cut in. "You sure know how to pick 'em."

"And all this brings us back to Indiana Normal and good old Burt," Alice summarized.

"I'm not sure. I'm so confused."

"So what happened after the kiss and the slap?" Alice needed to know.

"I got very angry, and I told him to take me straight home," Twinkles explained.

"Well," the interrogator pressed on for more details. "What was the mood like in the car before the kiss? Was he being aggressive with you?"

"Oh no," Twinkles was quick to reply. "He was very nice and gentle all evening. I was telling him about my breakup with Jefferey, and Burt was being very supportive."

"We were just sitting and talking, and then we were both quiet. Then, out of the blue, he closed his arm around me and kissed me."

"I was so shocked," she repeated. "We have been close before when we were alone like that but not romantically involved."

"Well," Alice reasoned out, "maybe you were not romantically involved, but it sure looks like he was. Haven't you ever wondered what it would be like if you and Burt were more than just friends?"

"Only once," Twinkles admitted. "It was last year at the Sadie Hawkins dance. You know, where the girls are supposed to ask the guys for a date."

"Yes, I know what a Sadie Hawkins dance is all about. Get on with the story," Alice broke in. "What happened?"

"Nothing really," the young lady calmly replied. "Except that we had a very sweet time that night, and after I got home that night, I started to wonder, what if…"

"But a few days later, I met Jefferey, and he was someone new and exciting."

"And poor old boring Burt got kicked aside," her friend accused.

"Well, not exactly like that, but yes, that is basically what happened."

"And how did Burt take it all?" Alice pressed on.

"You know Burt. He kind of shrugged it off, and then we were back to normal."

"Did anyone ever tell you that you are kind of heartless?" Alice asked.

"That's not a nice thing to say," Twinkles complained.

"I'll admit that it is probably more true than nice."

"It is getting late, and I have kept you up too long. I think that I had better go now," Twinkles said flatly.

Neither woman said another word as the late-night visitor headed for the door.

CHAPTER 22

Burt's *"Charger"* Comes Home It Was Spring of 1977

Burt Nickels was sitting at a forty-five-degree angle in his motorized bed that his father had leased for him the day he was released from the Valparaiso Indiana Hospital.

The modern mobilized bed had features that could allow Burt to lie flat on his back or gradually allow him to sit nearly upright.

Burt was painfully aware of his projected, painful journey back to even partial recovery.

Burt's new life consisted of daily visits from a physical therapist, who relentlessly put the young man through day after day of strengthening exercises designed to rehab and improve the function of knee and leg areas.

At Burt's continual pleading, he was able to convince his father to contract an auto moving company to transport the badly damaged auto wreckage to a spot in the Nickels' backyard.

From Burt's upstairs bedroom window, he was still able to see his once beautiful Charger while he slowly worked through the days and months of continual rehab.

On several occasions, Burt had received calls from other Dodge Charger owners seeking information about the overall condition of the badly damaged car. Some inquiries came with cash offers for the classic car. The engine, transmission, and other hard-to-find parts were worth big money in the right hands.

However, all such offers were simply rejected on the spot, because Burt could not witness the piece-by-piece destruction of his "pride and joy."

Soon the word got out that the classic wreck was not for sale.

As Burt was mulling over his future, a very familiar voice called up to him from the hallway below.

Ever since his release from the hospital, Twinkles had become a familiar voice in the Nickels' home.

Frow the time at the hospital when Burt kept calling her name, Burt and his family realized that the young lady's presence had a positive effect on his recovery.

"Are you decent?" Twinkles called up from the hallway below.

"Yes, of course," came the expected reply. Twinkles had been allowed access to Burt's bedroom, except when his physical therapist was with him.

Twinkles, casually dressed in a college mascot T-shirt and bright red shorts, was sure to attract the attention of her recovering friend. The colorful effect was not lost on the ailing patient. Burt gazed at the girl with wide-open eyes, managing to say only *wow*!

Twinkles tried not to show her appreciation for Burt's unspoken approval of her eye-catching outfit, but internally, she shared a smile with herself.

"So here you are, just like I left you yesterday. When are you going to get up and meet me at the top of the stairs?" she asked in jest.

"Give me about two years, tops?" he shot back.

"Not good enough," Twinkles shot back at him. "You should be running that Boston Marathon by next spring."

"Give me a break," Burt replied. "At least give me two years. By that time, I will not only run in that Yankee shindig, but I'll also win it."

One floor below, Mrs. Nickels cringed every time she heard Burt's persistent visitor berate and bully her injured son.

Every time she heard Twinkles speak so sharply to her helpless son, she would want to run upstairs and tell that young lady to leave her house and never come back.

But the deeply concerned mother could see the steady, inch-by-inch, daily improvement in her son's battle to improve his condition.

So for the sake of her son, she resolved not to interfere with whatever methods her son's close friend chose to employ—as long as it continued to yield positive results for her Burt.

CHAPTER 23

The Happy Kiss

"I'm beginning to believe that it is about time for someone to take you out of circulation, so to speak," Burt decided.

"And do you have anyone in mind who could qualify for this lofty position?" she asked, with a smile.

"I can only think of one, at this time," he came back.

"If you are referring to yourself," she teased, "then there is only one thing that I need to know."

"What, pray tell," he asked, mocking her, "could that possibly be."

"I'm still not sure about your kisses," she confessed. "You know that I only had that one."

"And what was wrong with my initial offering?" he demanded with a big grin.

"Well," she started, "that one kiss was almost wonderful, and powerful, but…"

"But what," Burt cut in.

"Well," she continued, "the kiss was also soft and tender, almost like a flower petal landing on my lips. Then you pulled away so quickly."

"That was because you were pushing me away. And then you were slapping me in the face, if you recall," he reminded her.

"But that was because it was so unexpected. You had never tried to kiss me before," she pointed out. "Later that night, in my room at home, I relived that moment over and over. I thought that after I slapped you, you would never ever want to speak to me ever again."

"I actually thought that it was a 'now or never' moment with you," he confessed. "Then later, in my car outside my house, I realized what I had done on the spur of the moment. I figured that I had just killed any chance of ever having any serious relationship with you."

"I think that it is totally unfair to base one's whole future on the basis of just one kiss," she declared.

"So you are suggesting that we try this kiss thing all over again?" he asked.

Twinkles replied with a coy smile, "It only seems fair. This could be a pivotal moment in both of our lives. We have to look at this moment seriously."

"Seriously? Yes, seriously," he concluded. "I'm inclined to agree. We don't want to make any mistakes here."

"A wrong decision here could haunt us for life," Twinkles concluded, as she brought her lips gently touching Burt's lips in a soft, gentle, lingering kiss.

Other works by Alfred C. Knoerzer Sr.

The Rollercoaster Life
Tropical Temptation
I Can't Make Her Laugh

ABOUT THE AUTHOR

Alfred C. Knoerzer Sr. is a native-born "Hoosier" who was born and raised on a farm in the corn and wheat belt.

After graduating high, this adventure-seeking young man enlisted in the US Army and chose to become a paratrooper so he could jump out of perfectly good airplanes.

He tended bar in a VFW bar, DJed on an AM radio station in California, and taught introductory psychology in the Philippines. He also used his military training to train Filipino factory workers to organize and man private fire brigades in factories, schools, and commercial businesses.

He married a cute and resourceful wife, Marites, and together they brought forth two talented sons: Alfred II, an electronics buff, and Christian, a seasoned percussionist.